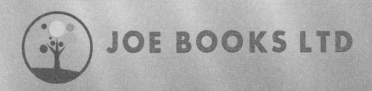

Copyright© 2016 Disney Enterprises, Inc. and Pixar Animation Studios. All rights reserved.

No portion of this publication may be reproduced or transmitted, in any form or by any means, without the express written permission of the copyright holders.

Published in the United States and Canada by Joe Books, Ltd.
567 Queen St W, Toronto, ON M5V 2B6
www.joebooks.com

Library and Archives Canada Cataloguing in Publication information is available upon request.
ISBN 978-1-98795-584-2 (Softcover edition)
ISBN 978-1-77275-297-7 (Ebook edition)

First Joe Books, Ltd. edition: June 2016

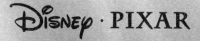

Disney · PIXAR

FINDING NEMO

CINESTORY COMIC

ADAPTATION, DESIGN, LETTERING, LAYOUT AND EDITING:
For Readhead Books:
Alberto Garrido, Ernesto Lovera, Puste, Ester Salguero,
Rocío Salguero, Eduardo Alpuente, Heidi Roux, Aaron Sparrow,
Heather Penner and Carolynn Prior.

SO, CORAL, WHEN YOU SAID YOU WANTED AN OCEAN VIEW, YOU DIDN'T THINK THAT WE WERE GONNA GET THE **WHOLE** OCEAN, DID YOU? HUH?

OH, YEAH. A FISH CAN **BREATHE** OUT HERE.

DID YOUR MAN DELIVER, OR DID HE **DELIVER**?

MY MAN DELIVERED.

AND IT WASN'T SO EASY.

BECAUSE A LOT OF OTHER CLOWNFISH HAD THEIR EYES ON THIS PLACE.

YOU BETTER BELIEVE THEY DID...

...EVERY SINGLE ONE OF THEM.

BUT MARLIN, I KNOW THAT THE DROP OFF IS DESIRABLE WITH THE GREAT SCHOOLS AND THE AMAZING VIEW AND ALL...

...BUT DO WE REALLY NEED SO MUCH SPACE?

CORAL, HONEY, THESE ARE OUR **KIDS** WE'RE TALKING ABOUT. THEY DESERVE THE BEST!

LOOK, LOOK, LOOK.

THEY'LL WAKE UP, POKE THEIR LITTLE HEADS OUT...

...AND THEY'LL SEE A **WHALE**! SEE, RIGHT BY THEIR BEDROOM WINDOW.

SHHH.

YOU'RE GONNA WAKE THE KIDS.

OH, RIGHT. RIGHT.

AWW, LOOK.

THEY'RE DREAMING.

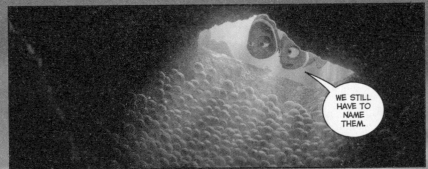

WE STILL HAVE TO NAME THEM.

NEMO? WELL, WE'LL NAME ONE NEMO, BUT I'D LIKE **MOST** OF THEM TO BE MARLIN JR.

JUST THINK THAT IN A COUPLE OF DAYS...

...WE'RE GONNA BE **PARENTS**!

YEAH!

WHAT IF THEY DON'T LIKE ME?

MARLIN.

NO, REALLY.

THERE'S OVER 400 EGGS. ODDS ARE, ONE OF THEM IS BOUND TO LIKE YOU.

WHAT?

YOU REMEMBER HOW WE MET?

WELL, I TRY NOT TO.

WELL, I REMEMBER. "EXCUSE ME, MISS, CAN YOU CHECK AND SEE IF I HAVE A HOOK IN MY LIP?"

MARLIN!

"OH, YOU GOTTA LOOK CLOSER BECAUSE IT'S WAY IN THERE."

GET AWAY!

HERE HE IS. CUTIE'S HERE!

WHERE DID EVERYBODY GO?

>GASP<
CORAL! GET
INSIDE THE
HOUSE,
CORAL.

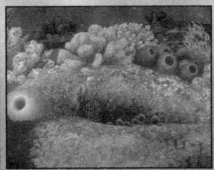

NO, CORAL, DON'T. THEY'LL BE FINE.

JUST GET INSIDE, YOU, RIGHT NOW.

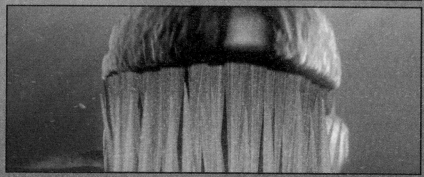

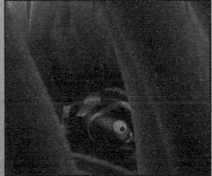

CORAL!

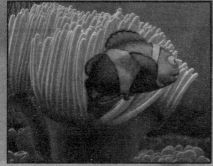

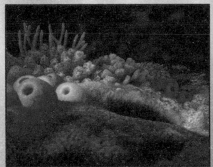

OHH... THERE, THERE, THERE.

IT'S OKAY, DADDY'S HERE. DADDY'S GOT YOU.

I PROMISE, I WILL NEVER LET ANYTHING HAPPEN TO YOU... NEMO.

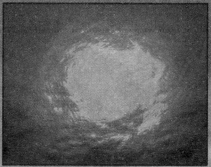

Walt Disney Pictures
presents

FIRST DAY OF SCHOOL!

FIRST DAY OF SCHOOL! WAKE UP, WAKE UP!

C'MON, FIRST DAY OF SCHOOL!

NOT YOU, DAD, **ME**! GET UP! GET UP!

I DON'T WANNA GO TO SCHOOL. FIVE MORE MINUTES.

IT'S TIME FOR SCHOOL! IT'S TIME FOR SCHOOL! IT'S TIME FOR SCHOOL! IT'S TIME FOR SCHOOL!

ALL RIGHT, I'M UP.

OH BOY!
OH BOY!
WHOA!

NEMO!

FIRST DAY
OF SCHOOL!

NEMO, DON'T
MOVE! **DON'T
MOVE!**

YOU'LL
NEVER GET
OUT OF THERE
YOURSELF.
I'LL DO IT.

NO.

ALL RIGHT,
WHERE'S
THE BREAK?
YOU FEEL A
BREAK?

SOMETIMES YOU CAN'T TELL 'CAUSE FLUID IS RUSHING TO THE AREA.

NOW, ANY RUSHING FLUIDS?

NO.

ARE YOU WOOZY?

NO.

HOW MANY STRIPES DO I HAVE?

I'M FINE.

ANSWER THE STRIPE QUESTION!

THREE.

NO! SEE, SOMETHING'S WRONG WITH YOU. I HAVE ONE, TWO, THREE--THAT'S ALL I HAVE?

OH, YOU'RE OKAY. HOW'S THE LUCKY FIN?

LUCKY.

LET'S SEE.

ARE YOU SURE YOU WANNA GO TO SCHOOL THIS YEAR? 'CAUSE THERE'S NO PROBLEM IF YOU DON'T. YOU CAN WAIT FIVE OR SIX YEARS.

COME ON, DAD. IT'S TIME FOR SCHOOL.

AH-AH-AH! FORGOT TO BRUSH.

DO YOU WANT THIS ANEMONE TO STING YOU?

OHH...

BRUSH.

YES.

BRUSH
BRUSH

OKAY, I'M DONE.

YOU MISSED A SPOT!

WHERE?

THERE. HA HA! RIGHT **THERE**. AND HERE AND HERE AND HERE!

DAD...

ALL RIGHT. COME ON, BOY.

DAD, MAYBE WHILE I'M AT SCHOOL, I'LL SEE A **SHARK**!

I HIGHLY DOUBT THAT.

HAVE YOU EVER **MET** A SHARK?

NO, AND I DON'T PLAN TO.

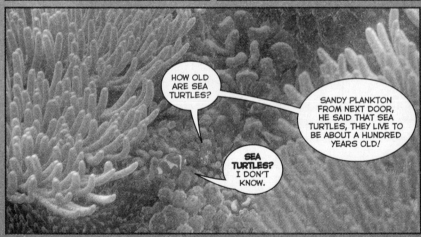

HOW OLD ARE SEA TURTLES?

SANDY PLANKTON FROM NEXT DOOR, HE SAID THAT SEA TURTLES, THEY LIVE TO BE ABOUT A HUNDRED YEARS OLD!

SEA TURTLES? I DON'T KNOW.

WELL, YOU KNOW WHAT, IF I EVER MEET A SEA TURTLE, I'LL ASK HIM. AFTER I'M DONE TALKING TO THE SHARK, OKAY?

WHOA, WHOA, WHOA! HOLD ON, HOLD ON, WAIT TO CROSS.

FWISH

HOLD MY FIN, HOLD MY FIN.

DAD, YOU'RE NOT GONNA FREAK OUT LIKE YOU DID AT THE PETTING ZOO, ARE YOU?

HEY, THAT SNAIL WAS ABOUT TO CHARGE. HMM, I WONDER WHERE WE'RE SUPPOSED TO GO.

BYE, MOM!

I'LL PICK YOU UP AFTER SCHOOL!

COME ON, YOU GUYS. **STOP IT! GIVE IT BACK!**

COME ON, WE'LL TRY OVER THERE.

WELL, LOOK WHO'S OUT OF THE ANEMONE.

EXCUSE ME, IS THIS WHERE WE MEET HIS TEACHER?

YES. SHOCKING, I KNOW.

MARTY, RIGHT?

MARLIN.

BOB.

TED.

BILL.

HEY, YOU'RE A CLOWNFISH. YOU'RE FUNNY, RIGHT? HEY, TELL US A JOKE.

YEAH, YEAH. COME ON, GIVE US A FUNNY ONE.

WELL, ACTUALLY, THAT'S A COMMON MISCONCEPTION. CLOWNFISH ARE NO FUNNIER THAN ANY OTHER FISH.

AW, COME ON, CLOWNIE.

YEAH, DO SOMETHING FUNNY.

YEAH!

ALL RIGHT, I KNOW ONE JOKE. UM, THERE'S A MOLLUSK, SEE? AND HE WALKS UP TO A SEA-- WELL HE DOESN'T WALK UP, HE SWIMS UP.

WELL, ACTUALLY THE MOLLUSK ISN'T MOVING. HE'S IN ONE PLACE AND THEN THE SEA CUCUMBER...

...WELL THEY--I MIXED UP. THERE WAS A MOLLUSK AND A SEA CUCUMBER. NONE OF THEM WERE WALKING, SO FORGET THAT I SAID THAT--

HA HA HA HA HA!

SHELDON!

GET OUT OF MR. JOHANSENN'S YARD, **NOW**!

ALL RIGHT, YOU KIDS! OOH! UUH, WHERE'D YOU GO? WHERE'D YOU GO? WHERE, WHERE'D YOU GO?

HA HA HA HA HA!

DAD, DAD... CAN I GO PLAY TOO? CAN I?

I WOULD FEEL BETTER IF YOU GO PLAY OVER ON THE SPONGE BEDS.

BOING BOING

PLOF

WAAAAAAH!

HE WAS BORN WITH IT, KIDS. WE CALL IT HIS **LUCKY** FIN.

DAD.

SEE THIS TENTACLE? IT'S ACTUALLY SHORTER THAN ALL MY OTHER TENTACLES. BUT YOU CAN'T REALLY TELL.

ESPECIALLY WHEN I TWIRL THEM LIKE THIS.

I'M H2O-INTOLERANT.

÷AH-CHOOO!÷

I'M OBNOXIOUS.

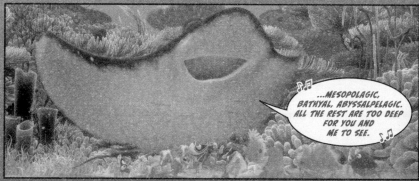

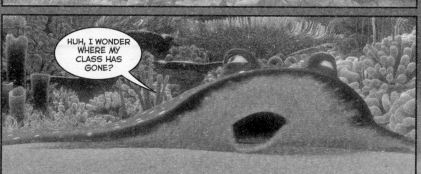

WE'RE UNDER HERE!

OH, **THERE** YOU ARE!

CLIMB ABOARD, EXPLORERS.

OH, KNOWLEDGE EXPLORING IS OH SO LYRICAL, WHEN YOU THINK THOUGHTS THAT ARE EMPIRICAL.

DAD, YOU CAN GO NOW.

DAD, IT'S TIME FOR YOU TO **GO** NOW.

JUST SO YOU KNOW, HE'S GOT A LITTLE FIN. I FIND IF HE'S HAVING TROUBLE SWIMMING, I LET HIM TAKE A BREAK. TEN, FIFTEEN MINUTES.

DON'T WORRY. WE'RE GONNA STAY TOGETHER AS A GROUP.

OKAY, CLASS, OPTICAL ORBITS UP FRONT. AND REMEMBER, WE KEEP OUR SUPRAESOPHOGEAL GANGLION TO OURSELVES... THAT MEANS **YOU**, JIMMY.

AW, MAN!

BYE, NEMO!

BYE, DAD!

BYE, SON.

BE SAFE.

HEY, YOU'RE DOING PRETTY WELL FOR A FIRST TIMER.

WELL, YOU CAN'T HOLD ON TO THEM FOREVER, CAN YOU?

YEAH, I HAD A TOUGH TIME WHEN **MY** OLDEST WENT OUT AT THE DROP OFF.

THEY JUST GOTTA GROW UP--THE DROP OFF?! **THEY'RE GOING TO THE DROP OFF?!**

WH-WHAT ARE YOU, **INSANE**?! WHY DON'T WE FRY 'EM UP NOW AND SERVE THEM WITH CHIPS!?

OH, LET'S NAME THE SPECIES, THE SPECIES, THE SPECIES. LET'S NAME THE SPECIES THAT LIVE IN THE SEA.

WHOA.

THERE'S PORIFERA, COELENTERATA, HYDROZOA, SCYPHOZOA, ANTHOZOA, CTENOPHORA, BRYOZOAS, THREE! GASTROPODA, ARTHROPODA, ECHINODERMA, AND SOME FISH LIKE YOU AND ME. COME ON, SING WITH ME. OH...!

JUST THE GIRLS THIS TIME.

OH, SEAWEED IS COOL. SEAWEED IS FUN. IT MAKES ITS FOOD FROM THE RAYS OF THE SUN...

OKAY, THE DROP OFF. ALL RIGHT, KIDS, FEEL FREE TO EXPLORE BUT STAY CLOSE.

≳GASP≲ STROMALITIC CYANOBACTERIA! GATHER. AN ENTIRE ECOSYSTEM CONTAINED IN ONE INFINITESIMAL SPECK. THERE ARE AS MANY PROTEIN PAIRS CONTAINED IN THIS...

COME ON, LET'S GO.

COME ON, SING WITH ME!

THERE'S PORIFERA, COELENTERA, HYDROZOA, SCYPHOZOA, ANTHOZOA, CTENOPHORA, BRYOZOAS, THREE!

HEY GUYS, WAIT UP!

WHOA.

WHAT'S THAT?

I KNOW WHAT THAT IS. OH, OH! SANDY PLANKTON SAW ONE. HE SAID IT WAS CALLED A... A BUTT.

OOH!!

WOW. THAT'S A PRETTY BIG BUTT.

OH, LOOK AT ME. I'M GONNA GO TOUCH THE BUTT. ⁒AH-CHOOO!⁒ WHOA!

⁒AH-CHOOO⁒

WHOA!

HA HA HA HA HA!

OH YEAH? LET'S SEE **YOU** GET CLOSER.

OKAY. BEAT THAT.

COME ON, NEMO. HOW FAR CAN YOU GO?

THIS DOES NOT CONCERN YOU, KIDS. AND YOU'RE LUCKY I DON'T TELL YOUR PARENTS YOU WERE OUT THERE.

YOU KNOW YOU CAN'T SWIM WELL.

I CAN SWIM **FINE**, DAD, **OKAY?**

NO, IT'S **NOT** OKAY. YOU SHOULDN'T BE ANYWHERE NEAR HERE. OKAY, I WAS RIGHT. YOU'LL START SCHOOL IN A YEAR OR TWO.

NO, DAD! JUST BECAUSE **YOU'RE** SCARED OF THE OCEAN--

CLEARLY, YOU'RE NOT READY. AND YOU'RE NOT COMING BACK HERE 'TIL YOU ARE. YOU **THINK** YOU CAN DO THESE THINGS BUT YOU JUST **CAN'T**, NEMO!

I HATE YOU.

THERE'S-- NOTHING TO SEE. GATHER, UH, OVER THERE.

EXCUSE ME, IS THERE ANYTHING I CAN DO? I AM A SCIENTIST, SIR. IS THERE ANY PROBLEM?

I'M SORRY. I DIDN'T MEAN TO INTERRUPT THINGS.

HE ISN'T A GOOD SWIMMER AND IT'S A LITTLE TOO SOON FOR HIM TO BE OUT HERE UNSUPERVISED.

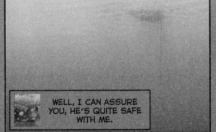

WELL, I CAN ASSURE YOU, HE'S QUITE SAFE WITH ME.

LOOK, I'M SURE HE IS. BUT YOU HAVE A LARGE CLASS AND HE CAN GET LOST FROM SIGHT IF YOU'RE NOT LOOKING.

I'M NOT SAYING YOU'RE NOT LOOKING--

GET BACK
HERE!

I SAID
GET BACK
HERE,
NOW!

STOP! YOU TAKE ONE
MORE MOVE, MISTER.
DON'T YOU DARE!

IF YOU PUT ONE FIN ON
THAT BOAT... ARE YOU
LISTENING TO ME?

DON'T TOUCH
THE BO--**NEMO!**

TAP

HE TOUCHED THE BUTT.

YOU JUST PADDLE YOUR LITTLE TAIL BACK HERE, NEMO. THAT'S RIGHT. YOU ARE IN **BIG TROUBLE**, YOUNG MAN. DO YOU HEAR ME? BIG...BIG--

BIG... BIG--

AAAAH!

AAAAH!

DADDY! HELP ME!

I'M COMING, NEMO!

-;GASP;-

GET UNDER ME, KIDS!

AAAAH!

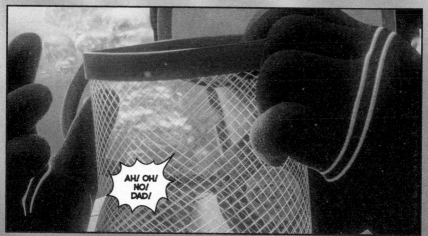

THE FLASH OF THE CAMERA BLINDS MARLIN...

AS MARLIN'S VISION BEGINS THE CLEAR, HE SEES THE DIVER SWIN TOWARD THE BOAT WITH HIS CAPTIVE SON...

NEMO, NO! NEMO!

NEMO! NEMO!

NEMO! NO!

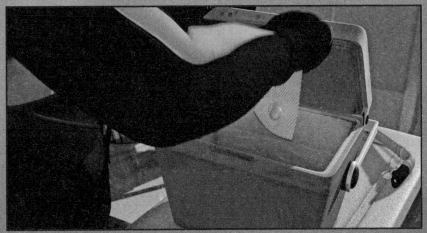

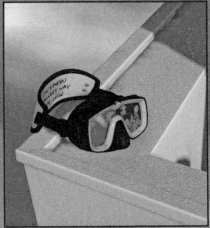

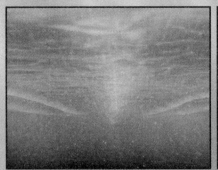

OH NO.
NO, NO.

IT'S GONE,
IT'S GONE. NO,
NO, IT **CAN'T** BE
GONE.

NO, **NO!**
NEMO! NEMO!
NEMO! NO!
NEMO! **NEMO!**
÷GASP!÷

NO,
PLEASE,
NO! NO,
NO!

BOFF

OOH, OOH...

OHH. OH, OH. SORRY! I DIDN'T SEE YOU. SIR, ARE YOU OKAY?

HE'S GONE, HE'S GONE..

THERE, THERE. IT'S ALL RIGHT.

HE'S GONE.

IT'LL BE OKAY.

NO, NO. THEY TOOK HIM AWAY. I HAVE TO FIND THE BOAT.

HEY, I'VE SEEN A BOAT.

YOU HAVE?

IT PASSED BY NOT TOO LONG AGO.

NO PROBLEM.

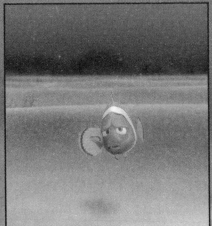

SUDDENLY, DORY DARTS AWAY!

SWOOOSH

HEY! WAIT!

WHSSSH

WILL YOU QUIT IT?

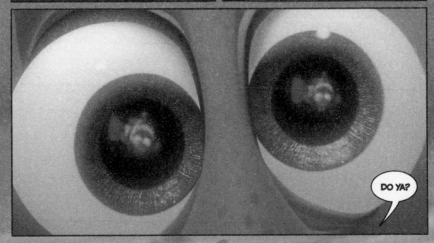

IT WENT THIS WAY, IT WENT THIS WAY. FOLLOW ME!

WAIT A MINUTE, WAIT A MINUTE! WHAT IS GOING ON? YOU ALREADY TOLD ME WHICH WAY THE BOAT WAS GOING!

I DID? OH NO...

IF THIS IS SOME KIND OF PRACTICAL JOKE, IT'S NOT FUNNY! AND I **KNOW** FUNNY...I'M A **CLOWNFISH**!

NO, IT'S NOT. I KNOW IT'S NOT. I'M SO SORRY. SEE, I SUFFER FROM SHORT-TERM MEMORY LOSS.

SHORT-TERM MEMORY LOSS. I DON'T **BELIEVE** THIS!

NO, IT'S TRUE. I FORGET THINGS ALMOST INSTANTLY. IT RUNS IN MY FAMILY... OR AT LEAST, I **THINK** IT DOES.

HMMM.. WHERE ARE THEY?

CAN I HELP YOU?

SOMETHING'S WRONG WITH YOU, REALLY. YOU'RE WASTING MY TIME. I HAVE TO FIND MY SON.

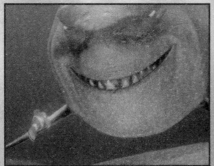

HELLO.

;GASP;

WELL, HI!

NAME'S BRUCE.

IT'S ALL RIGHT, I UNDERSTAND. WHY TRUST A **SHARK**, RIGHT?

HA HA HA HA HA HA HA!

SO, WHAT'S A COUPLE OF BITES LIKE YOU DOING OUT SO LATE, EH?

NOTHING. WE'RE NOT DOING ANYTHING. WE'RE NOT EVEN OUT.

GREAT! THEN HOW'D YOU MORSELS LIKE TO COME TO A LITTLE GET-TOGETHER I'M HAVIN'?

YOU MEAN LIKE A PARTY?

YEAH, YEAH, THAT'S RIGHT--A PARTY! WHAT DO YOU SAY?

OOH, I LOVE PARTIES! PARTIES ARE FUN!

PARTIES **ARE** FUN, AND IT'S TEMPTING BUT--

OH, COME ON, I **INSIST**.

OH, OKAY. THAT'S ALL THAT MATTERS.

HEY, LOOK-- BALLOONS! IT **IS** A PARTY!

HA HA HA! MIND YOUR DISTANCE, THOUGH. THOSE BALLOONS CAN BE A BIT DODGY.

YOU WOULDN'T WANT ONE OF THEM TO **POP.**

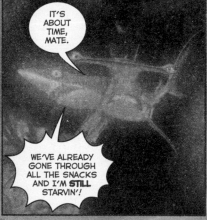

WE ALMOST HAD TO HAVE A FEEDING FRENZY.

COME ON, LET'S GET THIS OVER WITH.

RIGHT, THEN.

THE MEETING HAS OFFICIALLY COME TO ORDER. LET US ALL SAY THE PLEDGE.

"I AM A NICE SHARK, NOT A MINDLESS EATING MACHINE."

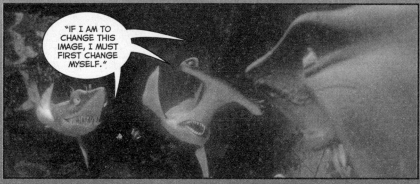

"IF I AM TO CHANGE THIS IMAGE, I MUST FIRST CHANGE MYSELF."

"FISH ARE FRIENDS, NOT FOOD."

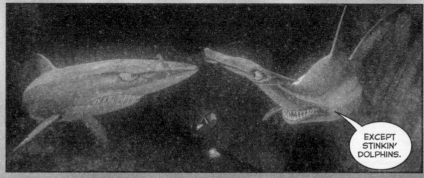

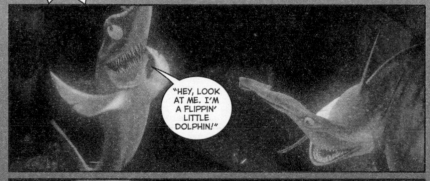

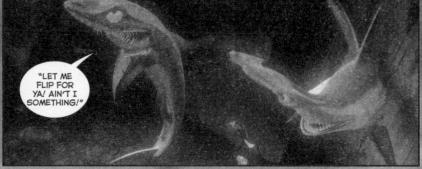

74

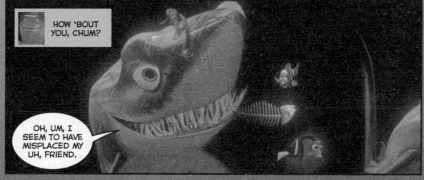

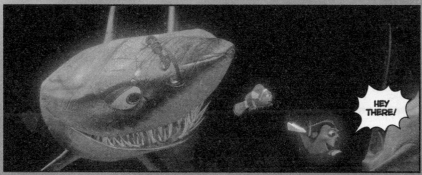

I HAD A FEELING THIS WOULD BE A DIFFICULT STEP. YOU CAN HELP YOURSELF TO ONE OF MY FRIENDS.

OH, THANKS, MATE. A LITTLE CHUM FOR CHUM, EH?

I'LL START THE TESTIMONIES. HELLO, MY NAME IS BRUCE.

HELLO, BRUCE.

IT HAS BEEN THREE WEEKS SINCE MY LAST FISH, ON MY HONOR, OR MAY I BE CHOPPED UP AND MADE INTO SOUP.

YOU'RE AN INSPIRATION TO ALL OF US.

CLAP

CLAP

AMEN.

76

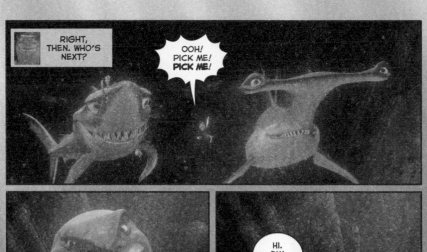

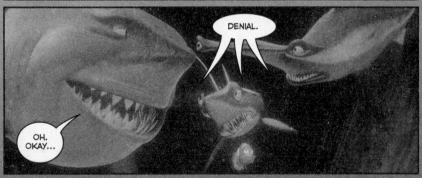

78

A CLOWNFISH? REALLY?!

OOH! I LOVE JOKES!

GO ON, TELL US A JOKE!

WELL I ACTUALLY **DO** KNOW ONE THAT'S PRETTY GOOD. THERE WAS THIS MOLLUSK AND HE WALKS UP TO A SEA CUCUMBER.

NORMALLY, THEY DON'T TALK, SEA CUCUMBERS, BUT IN A JOKE, EVERYONE TALKS.

SO THE SEA MOLLUSK SAYS...

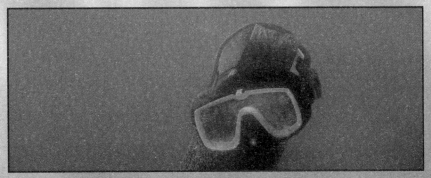

DADDY!

NEMO! NEMO!

NEMO! HA HA HA! NEMO! I DON'T GET IT.

FOR A CLOWNFISH, HE'S NOT THAT FUNNY.

I'M HAVIN' **FISH** TONIGHT!

REMEMBER THE **STEPS**, MATE!

JUST ONE BITE!

GOOD DAY! GRRR!

MARLIN AND DORY SWIM AS FAST AS THEY CAN, STAYING NARROWLY AHEAD OF BRUCE'S SNAPPING JAWS...

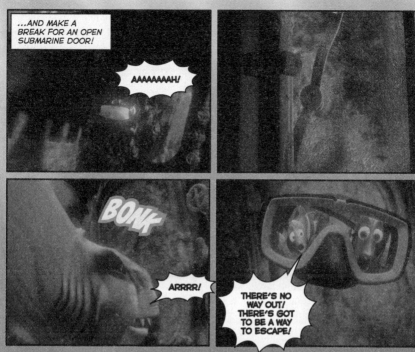

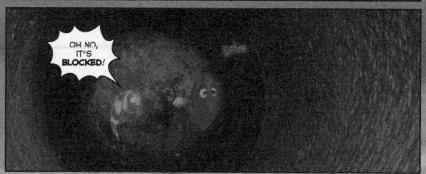

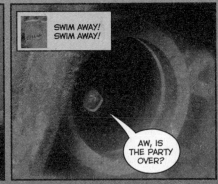

BARBARA?

UH-HUH?

PREP FOR HIS ANTERIOR CROWN, WOULD YOU, PLEASE? AND I'M GOING TO NEED A FEW MORE COTTON ROLLS.

OKAY.

HELLO, LITTLE FELLA!

AAH!

HEH HEH HEH! BEAUTY, ISN'T HE? I FOUND THAT GUY STRUGGLING FOR LIFE OUT ON THE REEF AND I SAVED HIM.

SO, HAS THAT NOVOCAINE KICKED IN YET?

AAAH! HE HASN'T BEEN **DECONTAMINATED** YET!

JACQUES!

CLEAN HIM!

OUI!

OUI.

OCEAN!

OOH, LA MER. BON.

VIP VIP VIP

VOILA. HE IS CLEAN.

HEY, NIGEL.

WHAT DID I MISS? AM I LATE?

ROOT CANAL. AND IT'S A DOOZY!

ROOT CANAL, EH? WHAT DID HE USE TO OPEN?

GATOR-GLIDDEN DRILL.

HE SEEMS TO BE FAVORING THAT ONE. HOPE HE DOESN'T GET SURPLUS SEALER AT THE PORTAL TERMINUS--

HELLO.

WHO'S THIS?

NEW GUY. HA HA HA!

THE DENTIST TOOK HIM OFF THE REEF.

WELL, MR. TUCKER, WHILE THAT SETS UP I'M GOING TO SEE A MAN ABOUT A WALLABY.

OH, DARLA.

WHAT? WHAT'S WRONG WITH HER?

SHE WOULDN'T STOP SHAKING THE BAG.

POOR CHUCKLES.

HE WAS HER PRESENT **LAST** YEAR.

HITCHED A RIDE ON THE PORCELAIN EXPRESS.

SHE'S A FISH KILLER.

OH!

JUST THINK ABOUT WHAT YOU NEED TO DO.

≀MPFMMMPPPFF!≀

COME ON.

≀MPFMMMPPPFF!≀

POP

PERFECT.

GOOD SQUIRMING! HA HA HA!

YAY!

YOU DID IT!

WOW. FROM THE OCEAN. JUST LIKE YOU, GILL.

YEAH.

I'VE SEEN **THAT** LOOK BEFORE. WHAT ARE YOU THINKING ABOUT?

I'M THINKING, TONIGHT, WE GIVE THE KID A **PROPER** RECEPTION.

SO KID, YOU GOT A NAME OR WHAT?

NEMO. I'M NEMO.

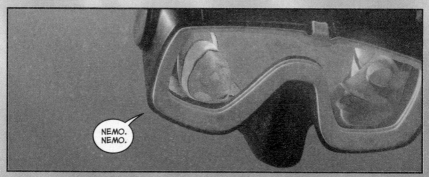

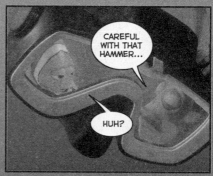

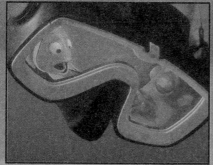

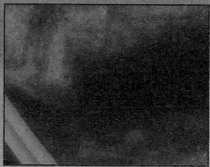

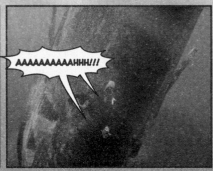

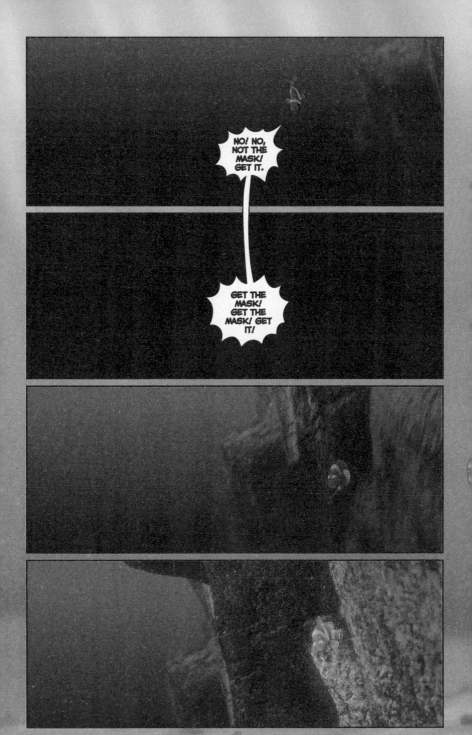

 DORY, DO YOU SEE ANYTHING?

 AAAH! SOMETHING'S GOT ME!

 THAT WAS ME. I'M SORRY.

 :GASPS: WHO WAS THAT?

 WHO COULD IT BE? IT'S ME!

 ARE... ARE YOU MY CONSCIENCE?

 YEAH. YEAH, I'M YOUR CONSCIENCE. WE HAVEN'T SPOKEN FOR A WHILE. HOW ARE YOU?

 HMM, CAN'T COMPLAIN.

 YEAH? GOOD. NOW, DORY. I WANT YOU TO TELL ME... DO YOU SEE ANYTHING?

 I SEE... I SEE A LIGHT.  A LIGHT?

 YEAH. OVER THERE.

HEY, CONSCIENCE. AM I DEAD?

 NO, I SEE IT TOO. WHAT IS IT?

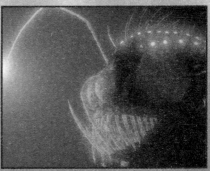

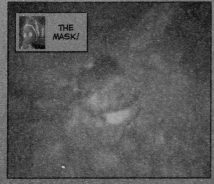

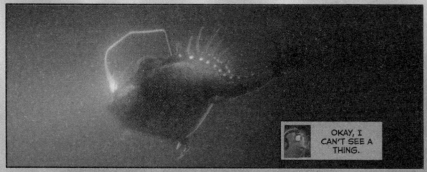

OKAY, I CAN'T SEE A THING.

OH, GEE!

HEY, LOOK! A MASK!

READ IT!

I'M SORRY, BUT IF YOU COULD JUST BRING IT A LITTLE CLOSER, I KIND OF NEED THE LIGHT.

THAT'S GREAT, KEEP IT RIGHT THERE.

OKAY, OKAY. MR. BOSSY.

JUST READ IT!

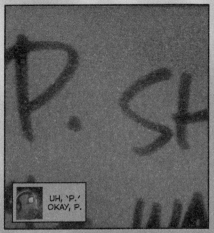

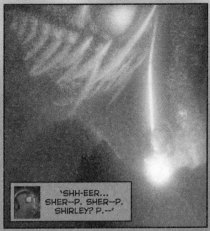

 LIGHT, PLEASE.

 'WALLA--WALLA--WALLA-BEEE...'

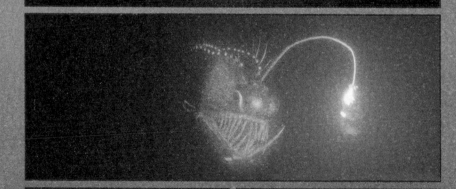

GLOMP

WAAH! WAAAH! WAAAAH!

THE SECOND LINE'S '42 WALLABY WAY!'

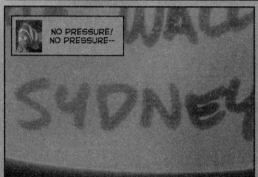

>ZZZZZZ<

TAP

>PSST.<
NEMO.

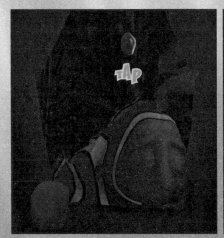

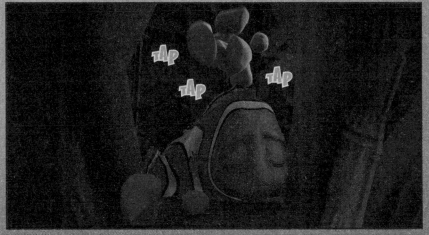

FROM THIS MOMENT ON, YOU WILL NOW BE KNOWN AS (SHARKBAIT).

SHARKBAIT! OOH HA HA!

YOU SEE THAT FILTER?

YEAH?

YOU'RE THE ONLY ONE WHO CAN GET IN AND OUT OF THAT THING.

WHAT WE NEED YOU TO DO IS TAKE A PEBBLE INSIDE...

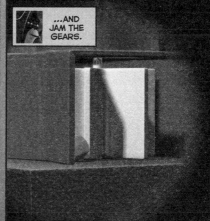

...AND JAM THE GEARS.

YOU DO THAT AND THIS TANK'S GONNA GET FILTHIER AND FILTHIER BY THE MINUTE.

PRETTY SOON, THE DENTIST'LL HAVE TO CLEAN THE TANK HIMSELF.

AND WHEN HE DOES, HE'LL TAKE US OUT OF THE TANK, PUT US IN THE INDIVIDUAL BAGGIES...

...THEN WE ROLL OURSELVES DOWN THE COUNTER, OUT THE WINDOW, OFF THE AWNING, INTO THE BUSHES...

...ACROSS THE STREET, AND INTO THE HARBOR!

IT'S **FOOLPROOF!** WHO'S WITH ME?

AYE!

AYE!

AYE!

AYE!

I THINK YOU'RE NUTS.

NO OFFENSE, KID, BUT, UM... YOU'RE NOT THE BEST SWIMMER.

HE'S FINE, HE CAN DO THIS. SO SHARKBAIT, WHAT DO YOU THINK?

LET'S DO IT.

AAAAAND THEY'RE GONE AGAIN. ⸱:SIGH:⸱

P. SHERMAN 42 WALLABY WAY, SYDNEY. WHY DO I HAVE TO TELL YOU OVER AND OVER AGAIN? I'LL TELL YOU AGAIN. I DON'T GET TIRED OF IT--

OKAY, ALL RIGHT.

HERE'S THE THING.

HUH?

UH-HUH.

YOU KNOW, I THINK IT'S JUST BEST IF I JUST...CARRY ON FROM HERE...BY MYSELF.

OKAY.

Y'KNOW, ALONE.

UH-HUH.

WITHOUT, WITHOUT..WELL, I MEAN, NOT WITHOUT YOU. I MEAN, IT'S JUST THAT I DON'T WANT YOU... WITH ME.

HUH?

I DON'T WANNA HURT YOUR FEELINGS.

YOU WANT ME TO LEAVE?

WAIT, WAIT, UM...

IT'S A SWORDFISH.

HEY, CLOWN BOY! LET THE LADY GUESS.

WHERE'S THE BUTTER?

OH-OH-OH! IT'S ON THE TIP OF MY TONGUE.

:-COUGH:- LOBSTER :-COUGH:-.

SAW THAT.

WHAT?

LOTS OF LEGS, LIVES IN THE OCEAN.

CLAM!

CLOSE ENOUGH!

♪♫ OH, IT'S A WHALE OF A TALE, I'LL TELL YOU LAD, A WHALE OF A TALE.

OH, THEY'RE GOOD.

WHAT'S THE MATTER? WHILE THEY'RE DOING THEIR SILLY LITTLE IMPRESSIONS, I AM MILES FROM HOME, WITH A FISH THAT CAN'T EVEN REMEMBER HER OWN NAME!

BOY, BET THAT'S FRUSTRATING.

YEAH! MEANWHILE MY SON IS OUT THERE.

YOUR SON CHICO?

NEMO.

RIGHT. GOT IT.

BUT IT DOESN'T MATTER, 'CAUSE NO FISH IN THIS ENTIRE OCEAN IS GONNA HELP ME.

WELL, I'M HELPING YOU. WAIT RIGHT HERE.

HEY, GUYS.

WHAT, IS HE BOTHERING YOU AGAIN?

NO, NO, HE'S A GOOD GUY. GO EASY ON HIM, HE'S LOST HIS SON, FABIO. ANY OF YOU HEARD OF P. SHERMAN, 42 WALLABY WAY, SYDNEY?

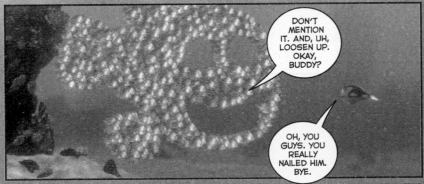

148

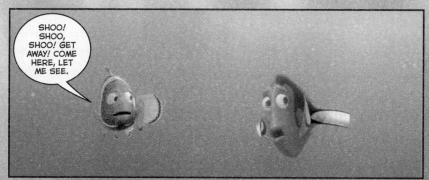

IT DOESN'T LOOK BAD, YOU'RE GONNA BE FINE. BUT NOW WE KNOW, DON'T WE?

YEAH.

THAT WE DON'T WANNA TOUCH THESE AGAIN. LET'S BE THANKFUL THIS TIME IT WAS JUST A LITTLE ONE.

AAAAH!

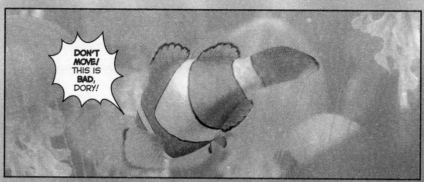

OOH! TWO IN A ROW, BEAT THAT.

DORY! ALL RIGHT, LISTEN TO ME. I HAVE AN IDEA, A GAME.

A GAME?

A GAME. YES.

AAH! I LOVE GAMES! PICK ME!

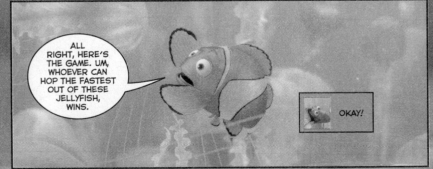

ALL RIGHT, HERE'S THE GAME. UM, WHOEVER CAN HOP THE FASTEST OUT OF THESE JELLYFISH, WINS.

OKAY!

RULES, RULES, RULES!

OKAY!

YOU CAN'T TOUCH THE TENTACLES, ONLY THE TOPS.

SOMETHING ABOUT TENTACLES, GOT IT. ON YOUR MARK, GET SET, GO!

W-WAIT! WAIT! NOT SOMETHING ABOUT THEM, IT'S ALL ABOUT THEM! WAIT!

WEEEE!

DORY!!

DORY!

GOTTA GO FASTER IF YOU WANNA WIN!

WAIT A MINUTE-- WHOA! DORY!

157

158

OUCH!

NO, YOU'RE DOING FINE! YOU'RE, YOU'RE ACTUALLY WINNING! BUT YOU GOTTA STAY AWAKE. UH, WHERE DOES P. SHERMAN LIVE?

UGGGHHH!

UGH...AM I DISQUALIFIED?

P... SHERMAN... WALLABY WAY... SYDNEY...

THAT'S IT!

MARLIN AND DORY MANAGE TO ESCAPE FROM THE JELLYFISH.

SYDNEY.

YOU MISS YOUR DAD, DON'T YOU, SHARKBAIT?

YEAH.

WELL, YOU'RE LUCKY TO HAVE SOMEONE OUT THERE WHO'S LOOKIN' FOR YOU.

HE'S NOT LOOKING FOR ME. HE'S SCARED OF THE OCEAN.

PEACH, ANY MOVEMENT?

HE'S HAD AT LEAST FOUR CUPS OF COFFEE, IT'S GOTTA BE SOON.

KEEP ON HIM.

POTTY BREAK! POTTY BREAK! HE JUST GRABBED THE READER'S DIGEST! WE HAVE 4.2 MINUTES.

THAT'S YOUR CUE, SHARKBAIT.

YOU CAN DO IT, KID.

OKAY, WE GOTTA BE QUICK. ONCE YOU GET IN, YOU SWIM DOWN TO THE BOTTOM OF THE CHAMBER AND I'LL TALK YOU THROUGH THE REST.

OKAY.

GO ON, IT'LL BE A PIECE OF KELP.

SPLASH

UH-HUH.

OKAY, INSIDE IT YOU'LL SEE A ROTATING FAN. VERY CAREFULLY, WEDGE THAT PEBBLE INTO THE FAN TO STOP IT TURNING.

SKREEZ

AAAH!

THAT'S IT, SHARKBAIT. NICE AND STEADY.

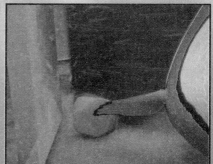

CLANK

PULL!

GILL, DON'T MAKE HIM GO BACK IN THERE.

NO.

WE'RE DONE.

THE SEA TURTLES, LIKE MANY OTHER FISH, USE THE FAST-MOVING E.A.C. TO QUICKLY TRAVERSE THE OCEAN!

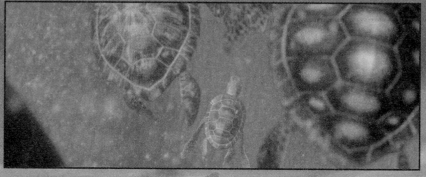

MARLIN WATCHES AS THE SMALLEST TURTLE SPINS OUT OF CONTROL...

SPLASH!

...AND OUT OF THE CURRENT!

OH MY GOODNESS!

WHOA.
KILL THE
MOTOR,
DUDE.

LET
US SEE
WHAT SQUIRT
DOES...

...FLYING
SOLO.

SPLASH!

BUT-BUT-BUT DUDE, HOW DO YOU KNOW WHEN THEY'RE READY?

WELL, YOU NEVER REALLY KNOW. BUT WHEN THEY KNOW, YOU'LL KNOW, YOU KNOW? HA.

HEY! LOOK, EVERYBODY!

I KNOW THAT DUDE. IT'S THE JELLYMAN.

WELL, GO ON, JUMP ON HIM.

TURTLE PILE!

W-W-WAI-WAIT--

194

WELL, OKAY. I LIVE ON THIS REEF, A LONG, LONG WAY FROM HERE.

OH, BOY. THIS IS GONNA BE GOOD, I CAN TELL.

AND MY SON, NEMO, HE WAS MAD AT ME. AND MAYBE HE WOULDN'T HAVE DONE IT IF I HADN'T BEEN SO TOUGH ON HIM... I DON'T KNOW.

ANYWAY, HE SWAM OUT IN THE OPEN WATER TO THIS BOAT AND WHEN HE WAS OUT THERE, THESE DIVERS APPEARED AND I TRIED TO STOP THEM BUT THE BOAT WAS TOO FAST.

SO WE SWAM OUT IN THE OCEAN TO FOLLOW IT...

...BUT HE COULDN'T STOP THEM. AND THEN NEMO'S DAD, HE SWIMS OUT TO THE OCEAN AND THEY BUMP INTO...

...THREE FEROCIOUS SHARKS! HE SCARES AWAY THE SHARKS BY BLOWIN' THEM UP!

AND THEN DIVES THOUSANDS OF...

GOLLY, THAT'S AMAZING!

...FEET STRAIGHT DOWN INTO THE DARK. IT'S LIKE *WICKED* DARK DOWN THERE, YOU CAN'T SEE A THING. AND THE ONLY THING THAT THEY CAN SEE DOWN THERE...

HEY, BOB!

...IS THE LIGHT FROM THIS BIG HORRIBLE CREATURE WITH RAZOR-SHARP TEETH. *NICE PARRY, OLD MAN.* AND THEN HE HAS TO BLAST HIS WAY...

...SO, THESE TWO LITTLE FISH HAVE BEEN SEARCHING THE OCEAN FOR DAYS. ON THE EAST AUSTRALIAN CURRENT...

...WHICH MEANS THAT HE MAY BE ON HIS WAY HERE RIGHT NOW. THAT SHOULD PUT THEM IN SYDNEY...

...HARBOR IN A MATTER OF DAYS. I MEAN, IT SOUNDS LIKE THIS GUY'S GONNA STOP AT...

...NOTHING UNTIL HE FINDS HIS SON. I SURE HOPE HE MAKES IT.

THAT'S ONE DEDICATED FATHER IF YOU ASK ME.

198

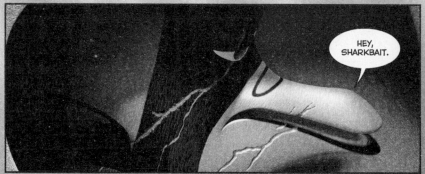

209

OH, YEAH!
HE'S TRAVELLED
HUNDREDS OF MILES.
HE'S BEEN BATTLING
SHARKS AND JELLYFISH
AND ALL SORTS
OF--

SHARKS?
THAT CAN'T
BE HIM.

ARE YOU
SURE? WHAT
WAS HIS NAME?
SOME SORT OF
SPORTFISH OR
SOMETHING: TUNA,
UH, TROUT...

MARLIN?

THAT'S **IT!** MARLIN! THE LITTLE CLOWNFISH FROM THE REEF.

IT'S MY DAD! HE TOOK ON A **SHARK!**

I HEARD HE TOOK ON **THREE.**

THREE SHARKS!?

THREE!?

THAT'S GOTTA BE FORTY-EIGHT HUNDRED TEETH!

YOU SEE, KID, AFTER YOU WERE TAKEN BY DIVER DAN OVER THERE, YOUR DAD FOLLOWED THE BOAT YOU WERE ON LIKE A MANIAC.

REALLY?

HE'S SWIMMING AND HE'S SWIMMING AND HE'S GIVING IT ALL HE'S GOT AND THEN THREE GIGANTIC SHARKS CAPTURE HIM AND HE BLOWS THEM UP!

AND THEN HE DIVES THOUSANDS OF FEET AND GETS CHASED BY A MONSTER WITH HUGE TEETH! HE TIES THIS THING TO A ROCK AND WHAT DOES HE GET FOR A REWARD? HE GETS TO BATTLE AN ENTIRE JELLYFISH FOREST!

AND NOW HE'S RIDING WITH A BUNCH OF SEA TURTLES ON THE EAST AUSTRALIAN CURRENT AND THE WORD IS HE'S HEADED THIS WAY RIGHT NOW, TO SYDNEY!

SHARKBAIT, YOU DID IT!

SHARKBAIT, YOU'RE...

...COVERED WITH GERMS! AAAAAAAH!!!

THAT TOOK GUTS, KID.

ALL RIGHT, GANG. WE HAVE LESS THAN 48 HOURS BEFORE DARLA GETS HERE. THIS TANK'LL GET PLENTY DIRTY IN THAT TIME, BUT WE HAVE TO HELP IT ALONG ANY WAY WE CAN.

JACQUES!

OUI!

NO CLEANING.

I SHALL RESIST.

ALL RIGHT, WE'RE HERE, DUDES! GET READY! YOUR EXIT'S COMIN' UP, MAN!

WHERE!? I DON'T SEE IT!

RIGHT THERE! I SEE IT! I SEE IT!

GOOD AFTERNOON, WE'RE GONNA HAVE A GREAT JUMP TODAY!

OKAY, SQUIRT HERE WILL NOW GIVE YOU A RUNDOWN OF PROPER EXITING TECHNIQUE!

OKAY, CRANK A HARD CUTBACK AS YOU HIT THE WALL! THERE'S A SCREAMING BOTTOM TURN, SO WATCH OUT! REMEMBER: RIP IT, ROLL IT, AND PUNCH IT!

IT'S LIKE HE'S TRYING TO SPEAK TO ME, I KNOW IT!

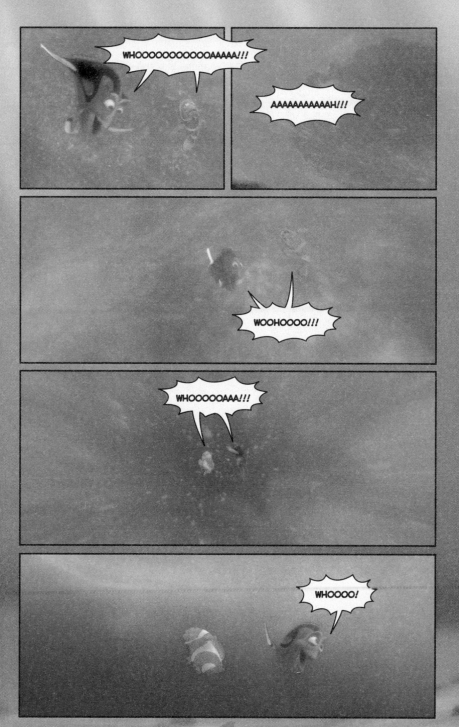

223

...ORANGE AND SMALL, AND WHITE STRIPES...

ME. AND THE NEXT ONE'S JUST A GUESS: ME.

OKAY, THAT'S JUST SCARY.

W-W-WAIT, I HAVE DEFINITELY SEEN THIS FLOATING SPECK BEFORE. THAT MEANS WE'VE PASSED IT BEFORE AND THAT MEANS WE'RE GOING IN CIRCLES AND THAT MEANS WE'RE NOT GOING STRAIGHT!

HEY. HEY!

WE GOTTA GET TO THE SURFACE, COME ON! LET'S FIGURE IT OUT UP THERE. LET'S GO! **FOLLOW ME!**

WHA--?

WHOA, WHOA, **WHOA!** HEY! RELAX.

TAKE A DEEP BREATH.

HEY! EXCUSE--

DORY! DORY! DORY! OKAY, NOW IT'S MY TURN. I'M THINKING OF SOMETHING DARK AND MYSTERIOUS. IT'S A FISH WE DON'T KNOW. AND IF WE ASK IT DIRECTIONS, IT COULD INGEST US AND SPIT OUT OUR BONES!

WHAT IS IT WITH MEN AND ASKING FOR DIRECTIONS?

LOOK, I DON'T WANNA PLAY THE GENDER CARD RIGHT NOW. YOU WANNA PLAY A CARD? LET'S PLAY THE 'LET'S NOT DIE' CARD.

YOU WANNA GET OUTTA HERE, DON'T YOU?

OF COURSE, I DO.

WELL THEN, HOW ARE WE GONNA DO THAT UNLESS WE GIVE IT A SHOT AND HOPE FOR THE BEST? HMMM? HMMMM!?

COME ON, TRUST ME ON THIS.

DORY, YOU DON'T FULLY UNDERSTAND...

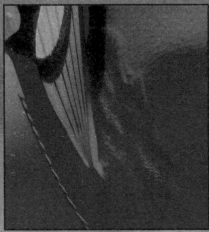

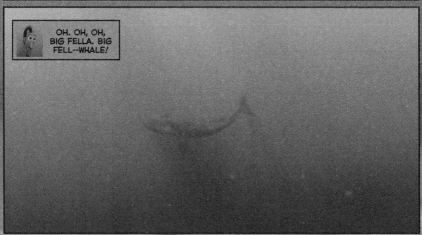

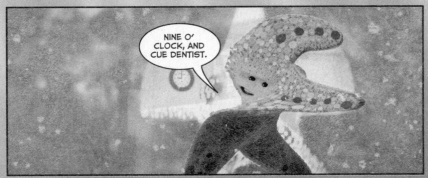

OKAY. WALKS TO THE COUNTER, DROPS THE KEYS...

BLOAT, THAT'S **DISGUSTING!**

TASTES PRETTY GOOD TO ME.

⊰BUUUURP⊱

EWW! DON'T YOU PEOPLE REALIZE WE ARE SWIMMING IN OUR OWN--

SHHH! HERE HE COMES.

CRIKEY, WHAT A STATE.

OH BARBARA, WHAT'S MY EARLIEST APPOINTMENT TOMORROW?

TEN O' CLOCK.

LEAVE IT OPEN, WOULD YOU? I GOTTA CLEAN THE FISH TANK BEFORE DARLA GETS HERE.

HEE HEE! DID YOU HEAR THAT, SHARKBAIT?

YAY! HE'S GONNA CLEAN THE TANK! HE'S GONNA CLEAN THE TANK! WE'RE GONNA BE CLEAN!

ARE YOU READY TO SEE YOUR DAD, KID?

UH-HUH.

OF COURSE YOU ARE. Y'KNOW, I WOULDN'T BE SURPRISED IF HE'S OUT THERE IN THE HARBOR WAITIN' FOR YOU RIGHT NOW.

YEAH.

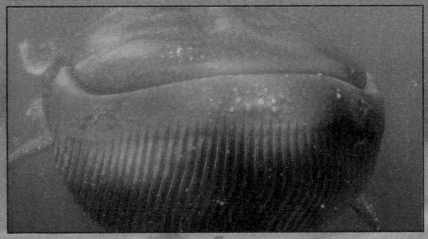

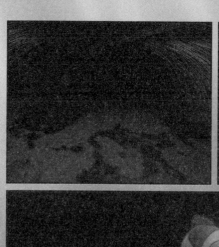

HA--HAAA--HAAAAAAAH!
WHOOO!

AAAAAAAAAAAH!

POF

WHOOO!

WOULD YOU JUST STOP IT?!

HERE COMES A BIG ONE--WHOOOOOOO! COME ON, YOU GOTTA TRY THIS!

WHY? WHAT'S WRONG?

WE'RE IN A WHALE! DON'T YOU GET IT?!

A WHALE?

A WHALE! 'CAUSE YOU HAD TO ASK FOR HELP! AND NOW WE'RE STUCK HERE!

WOW. A WHALE. YOU KNOW, I SPEAK WHALE.

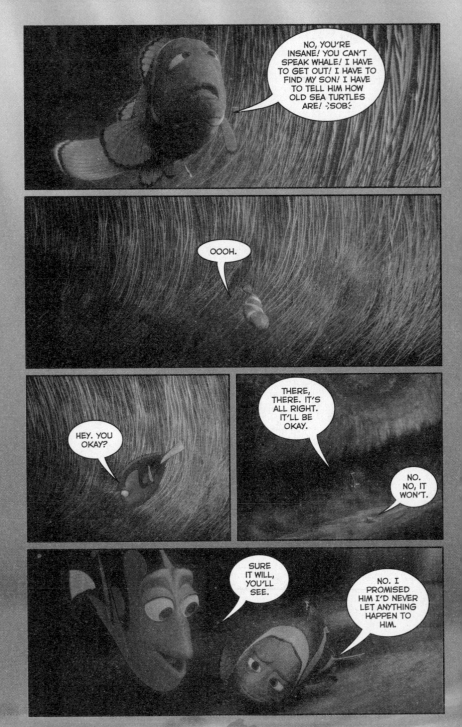

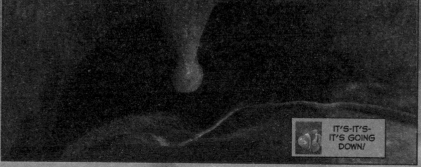

REALLY? YOU SURE ABOUT THAT?

LOOK, IT'S ALREADY HALF EMPTY!

HMM... I'D SAY IT'S HALF FULL.

STOP THAT! IT'S HALF EMPTY!

GSHAAAAAAAAAAAI

OKAY, THAT ONE WAS A LITTLE TOUGHER. HE EITHER SAID WE SHOULD GO TO THE BACK OF THE THROAT OR HE WANTS A ROOT BEER FLOAT.

OF COURSE HE WANTS US TO GO THERE! THAT'S EATING US!

HOW DO I TASTE, MOBY?! HUH?! DO I TASTE GOOD?! YOU TELL HIM I'M NOT INTERESTED IN BEING LUNCH!

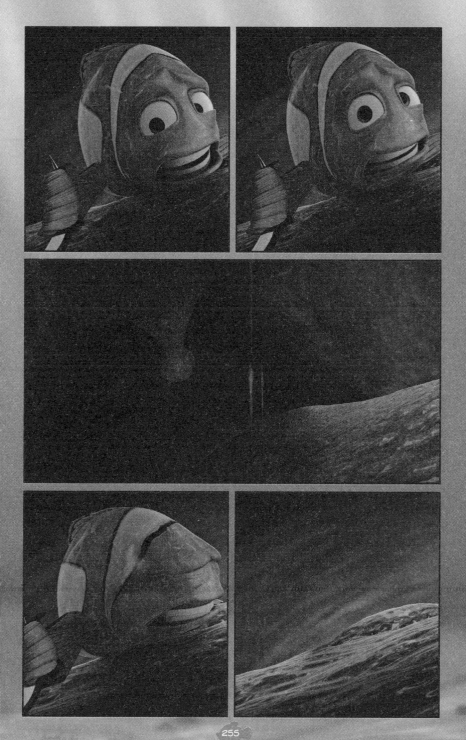

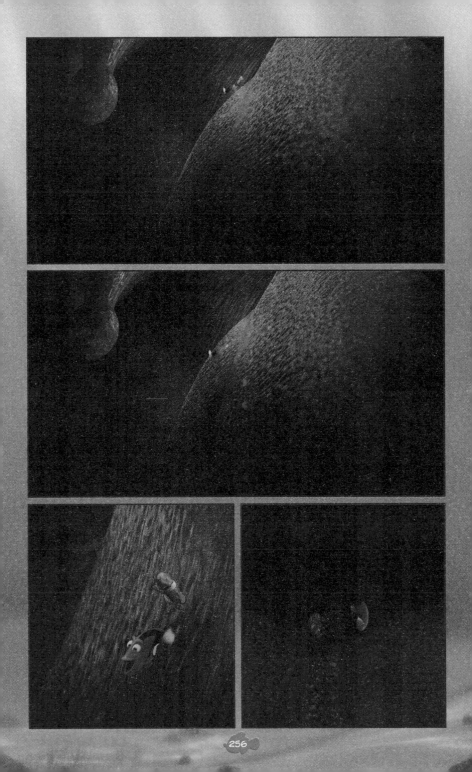

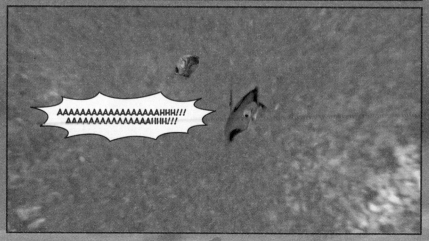

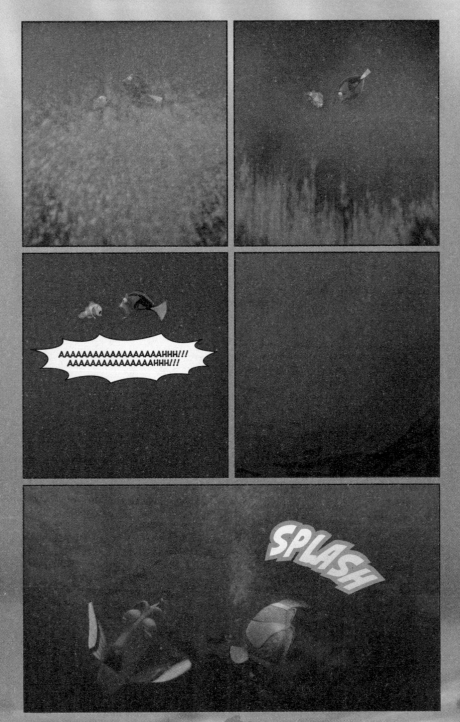

HA HA HA! WE'RE **ALIVE!**

LOOK! SY-D-NEY...

SYDNEY!

SYDNEY AGAIN!

IT'S MORNING, EVERYONE! TODAY'S THE DAY! THE SUN IS SHINING, THE TANK IS CLEAN AND WE ARE GETTING OUT OF--

⸖GASP⸖ --THE TANK IS CLEAN. **THE TANK IS CLEAN!**

BOSS MUST'VE INSTALLED IT LAST NIGHT WHILE WE WERE SLEEPIN'.

WHAT'RE WE GONNA DO?

BUT HOW?

WHAT'S IT SAY, PEACH?

THE AQUASCUM TWO-THOUSAND..

I CAN'T HEAR YOU, PEACH.

'THE AQUASCUM 2003 IS AN ALL-PURPOSE, SELF-CLEANING MAINTENANCE-FREE SALT WATER PURIFIER THAT IS GUARANTEED TO EVEN EXTEND THE LIFE OF YOUR AQUARIUM FISH.'

STOP IT!

'THE AQUASCUM IS PROGRAMMED TO SCAN YOUR TANK ENVIRONMENT EVERY FIVE MINUTES?'

SCAN? WHAT DOES THAT MEAN?

POOF

TEMPERATURE: 82 DEGREES. PH BALANCE: NORMAL.

OOOOOH.

DON'T FLUSH

NICE.

CURSE YOU, AQUASCUM!

THAT'S IT FOR THE ESCAPE PLAN. IT'S **RUINED!**

THEN WHAT'RE WE GONNA DO ABOUT--

DING

DARLA!

STAY DOWN, KID!

FALSE ALARM.

MY NERVES CAN'T TAKE MUCH MORE OF THIS.

WHAT'RE WE GONNA DO WHEN THAT LITTLE BRAT GETS HERE?

I'M THINKIN', I'M THINKIN'.

AAAH! OH! GILL!

NEMO!

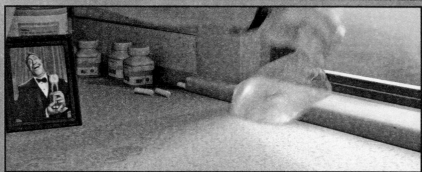

WHOOPS. **THAT** WOULD BE A NASTY FALL.

DING

DARLA!

ALL RIGHT, DO ANY OF THESE BOATS LOOK FAMILIAR TO YOU?

NO, BUT THE BOAT HAS TO BE HERE SOMEWHERE!

COME ON, DORY, WE'RE GONNA FIND IT.

I'M TOTALLY EXCITED. ÷YAWN÷

ARE YOU EXCITED? ÷YAWN÷

DORY, WAKE UP, WAKE UP. COME ON.

·GHHK·

·GHHK·
·GHHK·

HOT DOGS   SNACKS   FI   COLD

HEY, HEY, NIGEL. HEH, WOULD YOU LOOK AT THAT?

HUH? WHA-WHAT?

SUN'S BARELY UP AND ALREADY GERALD'S HAD MORE THAN HE CAN HANDLE.

YEAH. RECKON SOMEBODY OUGHTA HELP THE POOR GUY.

YEAH, YEAH, RIGHT.

WELL, DON'T EVERYBODY FLY OFF AT ONCE.

ALL RIGHT, GERALD, WHAT IS IT? FISH GOT YOUR TONGUE?

AAAAAAAAAAAAAAH!!!

NO. I KNOW YOUR SON. HE'S ORANGE, HE'S GOT A GIMPY FIN ON ONE SIDE...

THAT'S NEMO!

MINE! MINE! MINE! MINE! MINE! MINE!

AAAAH!!!

MINE! MINE! MINE! MINE! MINE! MINE!

AAAAAAAAAAAAAAH!!!

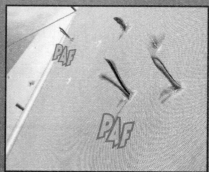

AAAAH! TOO LOUD! TOO LOUD FOR ME!

♪♫ TWINKLE, TWINKLE LITTLE STAR.

FIND A HAPPY PLACE, FIND A HAPPY PLACE, FIND A HAPPY PLACE!

DARLA, YOUR UNCLE WILL SEE YOU NOW.

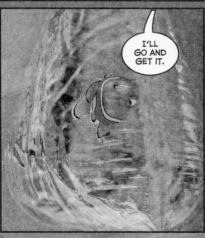

HEY! **HEY!** I FOUND HIS DAD!

WHERE'S **NEMO**?! WHERE IS HE?!

HE'S OVER THERE!

DENTIST! DENTIST!

WHAT'S A DENTIST?! WHAT IS THAT?! ÷GASP÷

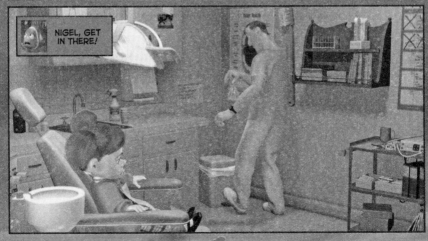

NIGEL, GET IN THERE!

I CAN'T GO IN THERE.

OH YES, YOU CAN! **CHARGE!**

WAAAAAAH!!

WHAT THE--?!

AAAAAAAAAAAH!

RING OF FIRE!

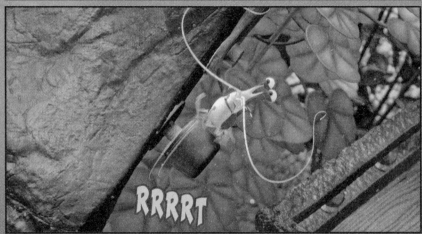

RRRRt

FISHY!

AAAAAAAAAH!

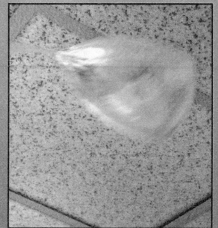

SPLASH!

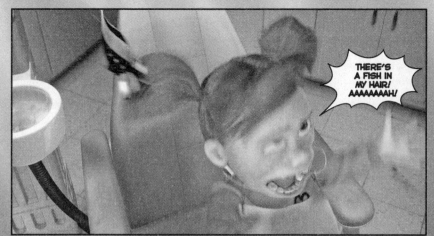

WITH THAT, GILL LEAPS...

...AND COMES BACK DOWN, LAUNCHING NEMO INTO THE AIR...

...SENDING HIM FLYING INTO THE SINK!

FSSH

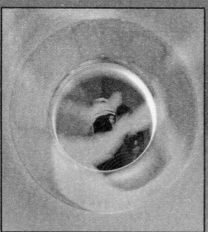

GO GET 'EM.

:GASP: OHHH!

HE DID IT! HA HA!

YAY!

I'M SO HAPPY!

IS HE GONNA BE OKAY, GILL?

DON'T WORRY. ALL DRAINS LEAD TO THE OCEAN.

FISHY?

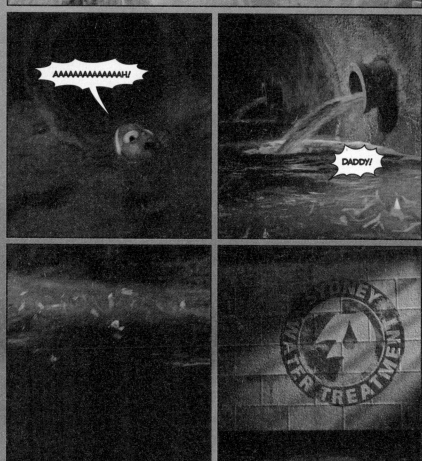

I'M, I'M SO SORRY.

TRULY, I AM.

HEY...

SUDDENLY, NEMO POPS OUT OF THE PIPE!

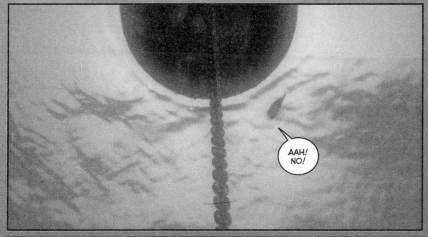

S-SS-SYL--
SHI--

SYDNEY.

'P. SHERMAN,
42 WALLABY WAY,
SYDNEY.'

'P. SHERMAN,
42 WALLABY WAY,
SYDNEY.'

'P. SHERMAN,
42 WALLABY WAY,
SYDNEY.'

'P. SHERMAN,
42 WALLABY WAY,
SYDNEY.'

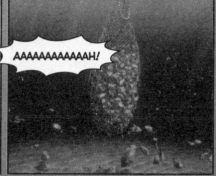

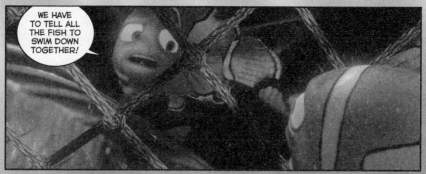

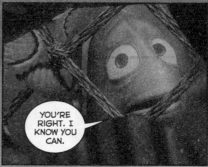

IT'S WORKING!

♫♪ KEEP SWIMMING! JUST KEEP SWIMMING! KEEP SWIMMING! ♫♪

JUST KEEP SWIMMING! KEEP SWIMMING!

COME ON, DAD!

YOU'RE DOING GREAT, SON!

KEEP SWIMMING! KEEP SWIMMING!

HRRNK

KEEP SWIMMING! KEEP SWIMMING!

CLACK

SPLASH!

...UNTIL FINALLY, IT BREAKS FREE!

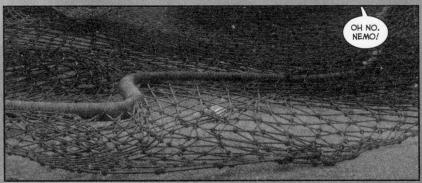

OH, THANK GOODNESS.

DAD...I DON'T HATE YOU.

NO, NO, NO. I'M SO SORRY, NEMO.

HEY, GUESS WHAT?

WHAT?

SEA TURTLES? I MET ONE! AND HE WAS A HUNDRED AND FIFTY YEARS OLD.

HUNDRED AND FIFTY?

YEP.

'CAUSE SANDY PLANKTON SAID THEY ONLY LIVE TO BE A HUNDRED.

SANDY PLANKTON? DO YOU THINK I WOULD CROSS THE ENTIRE OCEAN AND NOT KNOW AS MUCH AS SANDY PLANKTON?!

HA HA HA HA!

HE WAS A HUNDRED AND FIFTY! NOT ONE HUNDRED! WHO IS THIS SANDY PLANKTON THAT KNOWS EVERYTHING WRONG?

SOME TIME LATER.

TIME FOR SCHOOL! TIME FOR SCHOOL!

GET UP! LET'S GO! GO!

I'M GONNA WIN!

NO, YOU'RE NOT!

I DID IT! WOOHOO! HA HA HA!

OH! MY OWN SON BEATS ME.

CLIMB ABOARD, EXPLORERS!

338

THANKS, GUYS.

WELL, WE'LL SEE YOU NEXT WEEK.

KEEP UP WITH THE PROGRAM, DORY.

REMEMBER: FISH ARE FRIENDS...

...NOT FOOD! BYE!

HOLD ON! HERE WE GO! NEXT UP, KNOWLEDGE!

BYE, SON! HAVE FUN!

BYE, DAD!

OH! OH, MR. RAY! WAIT. I FORGOT SOMETHING.

LOVE YOU, DAD.

I LOVE YOU TOO, SON.

UH, DAD, YOU CAN LET GO NOW.

SORRY!

NOW GO HAVE AN ADVENTURE!

the end

for Glenn McQueen
1960 - 2002

343

DIRECTED BY
Andrew Stanton

CO-DIRECTED BY
Lee Unkrich

PRODUCED BY
Graham Walters

EXECUTIVE PRODUCER
John Lasseter

ASSOCIATE PRODUCER
Jinko Gotoh

ORIGINAL STORY BY
Andrew Stanton

SCREENPLAY BY
Andrew Stanton
Bob Peterson
David Reynolds

MUSIC BY
Thomas Newman

STORY SUPERVISORS
Ronnie del Carmen
Dan Jeup
Jason Katz

FILM EDITOR
David Ian Salter

SUPERVISING TECHNICAL DIRECTOR
Oren Jacob

PRODUCTION DESIGNER
Ralph Eggleston

DIRECTORS OF PHOTOGRAPHY
Sharon Calahan
Jeremy Lasky

SUPERVISING ANIMATOR
Dylan Brown

ART DIRECTORS
CHARACTERS
Ricky Vega Nierva
SHADING
Robin Cooper
ENVIRONMENTS
Anthony Christov
Randy Berrett

CG SUPERVISORS
CHARACTERS
Brian Green
OCEAN UNIT
Lisa Forssell
Danielle Feinberg

CG SUPERVISORS
REEF UNIT
David Eisenmann
TANK UNIT
Jesse Hollander
SHARKS/SYDNEY UNIT
Steve May

CG SUPERVISORS
GLOBAL TECHNOLOGY
Michael Fong
RENDERING
Anthony A. Apodaca
SHOT INTEGRATION
Michael Lorenzen

PRODUCTION MANAGER
Lindsey Collins

SOUND DESIGNER
Gary Rydstrom

344

CASTING

Mary Hidalgo
Kevin Reher
Matthew Jon Beck

CAST

Marlin	Albert Brooks	Nigel	Geoffrey Rush
Dory	Ellen DeGeneres	Crush	Andrew Stanton
Nemo	Alexander Gould	Coral	Elizabeth Perkins
Gill	Willem Dafoe	Squirt	Nicholas Bird
Bloat	Brad Garrett	Mr. Ray	Bob Peterson
Peach	Allison Janney	Bruce	Barry Humphries
Gurgle	Austin Pendleton	Anchor	Eric Bana
Bubbles	Stephen Root	Chum	Bruce Spence
Deb (& Flo)	Vicki Lewis	Dentist	Bill Hunter
Jacques	Joe Ranft	Darla	LuLu Ebeling
		Tad	Jordy Ranft
		Pearl	Erica Beck
		Sheldon	Erik Per Sullivan
		Fish School	John Ratzenberger

PRODUCTION SUPERVISOR
Marcia Gwendolyn Jones

STORY

STORY MANAGER
Blake Tucker

STORY ARTISTS
Jim Capobianco   Joseph "Rocket" Ekers
Bruce M. Morris   Peter Sohn
Nathan Stanton

ADDITIONAL STORYBOARDING
James S. Baker   Max Brace
Rob Gibbs   Matthew Luhn

DIGITAL STORYBOARDING
Courtney Booker

STORY CONSULTANT
Will Csaklos

STORY COORDINATOR
Rachel Raffael-Gates
Adam Bronstein

STORY PRODUCTION ASSISTANT
Romney T. Marino

ART

ART MANAGER
Doug Nichols

CHARACTER DESIGN
Dan Lee

ADDITIONAL CHARACTER DESIGN
Jason Deamer

PRODUCTION ARTISTS
Nelson "Rey" Bohol   David Fulp
Ellen Moon Lee   Albert Lozano
Nathaniel McLaughlin   James Pearson
Peter Sohn   Bud Thon

SCULPTORS
Jerome Ranft
Greg Dykstra

LEAD CG PAINTER
Belinda Van Valkenburg

CG PAINTERS
Bert Berry   Jamie Frye
Yvonne Herbst   Glenn Kim
Laura Phillips   Andrea Warren

VISUAL DEVELOPMENT
Geefwee Boedoe   Peter Deseve
Tony Fucile   Carter Goodrich
D. J. Cleland-Hura   George Hull
Dominique Louis   Simon Varela
Mark Whiting   Bruce Zick

ADDITIONAL VISUAL DEVELOPMENT
Rikki Cleland-Hura

ART COORDINATOR
Bert Berry

EDITORIAL

SUPERVISING FILM EDITOR
Lee Unkrich

SECOND FILM EDITORS
Katherine Ringgold
Stan Webb
Kevin Nolting

FIRST ASSISTANT EDITOR
Axel Geddes

SECOND ASSISTANT EDITORS
Luis Alvarez y Alvarez   Jason Hudak
David Suther   Elizabeth Thomas

TEMP MUSIC EDITOR
David Slusser

UNIT COORDINATOR
Pamela Darrow

OCEAN UNIT

UNIT MANAGER
Michael Warch

LEADS
Liz Kupinski Carter	Jun Han Cho
Scott G. Clifford	Derek Williams

CG ARTISTS
Cortney Armitage	Airton Dittz, Jr.
Louis Gonzales	Stefan Gronsky
Jae H. Kim	Keith Daniel Klohn
Mike Krummhoefener	Tom Miller
Amy Moran	David Munier
Jack Paulus	Justin Ritter
Apurva Shah	Erik Smitt
Michael L. Stein	Maria Yershova

UNIT COORDINATOR
Marcia Savarese

REEF UNIT

UNIT MANAGER
Kim Collins

LEADS
Robert Anderson
Don Schreiter
Kim White

CG ARTISTS
Jessica Abroms	Chris Bernardi
Simon Dunsdon	Steven James
Sungyeon Joh	Michael Kilgore
David MacCarthy	Michael K. O'Brien
Eileen O'Neill	Lisa Kim
Burt Peng	Andrew Pienaar
Timothy Swec	Sophie Vincelette
Brad Winemiller	

UNIT COORDINATORS
Suzanne Hightower-Purcell
Seth Murray

SHARKS/SYDNEY UNIT

UNIT MANAGER
Siouxsie Stewart

LEADS
Michael Fu
Ken Lao
Derek Williams

CG ARTISTS
Brian Boyd	Chris Chapman
Jun Han Cho	Kevin Edwards
Christina Garcia	Christina Haaser
Jean-Claude J. Kalache	Steven Kani
Keith Daniel Klohn	Ivo Kos
Holly Lloyd	Martin Nguyen
Kelly O'Connell	Phat Phuong
Gabriel Schlumberger	Suzanne Slatcher
Peter Sumanaseni	Erdem Taylan

UNIT COORDINATOR
Sheri Patterson

TANK UNIT

UNIT MANAGER
Michael Warch

LEADS
Brad Andalman
Scott G. Clifford
Sylvia Wong

PRODUCTION

PRODUCTION ACCOUNTANT	**Nephi Sanchez**
SCHEDULING COORDINATOR	**Heidi Cruz**
DIRECTOR OF PRODUCTION FINANCE	**Robert Taylor**
SUPERVISOR OF PRODUCTION RESOURCES	**Susan T. Tatsuno**
ASSISTANT PRODUCTION ACCOUNTANT	**Kesten Migdal**
ASSISTANT TO THE PRODUCER	**Marguerite K. Enright**
ASSISTANT TO THE DIRECTORS	**Lisa Marie Schwartz**
PRODUCTION OFFICE ASSISTANTS	**Jon Darrell Handy**
	Peter T. Schreiber
DISNEY PRODUCTION REPRESENTATIVE	**Jenny Aleman-Holman**

ADDITIONAL PRODUCTION SUPPORT

Cindy Cosenzo	**Xanthe Hohalek**	**Jennifer Kinavey**
Susan E. Levin	**David Lortsher**	**Julie McDonald**
Wendi McNeese	**Roger Noyes**	**Adrian Ochoa**
Karen Paik	**Marc Prager**	**Dan Sokolosky**

INFORMATION SYSTEMS

MANAGERS & LEADS

Peter Kaldis	**Erik Forman**
Alisa Gilden	**May Pon**
Alex Stahl	**Christopher C. Walker**
Warren Hays	

SYSTEMS ADMINISTRATORS & SUPPORT

Domenic Allen	**Neftali "El Magnifico" Alvarez**
James Bartel	**Jennifer Becker**
Gabriel Benveniste	**Bryan Bird**
Sean Brennan	**Lars R. Damerow**
james g. dashe	**Ross Dickinson**
Miles Egan	**Edward Escueta**
Sandy Falby	**Grant Gatzke**
Joshua Grant	**Bethany Jane Hanson**
Jason B. Hendrix	**Ling Hsu**
Kenneth "Yo" Huey	**Jason "Jayfish" Hull**
Jose "Gayle" Ignacio	**Humera Yasmin Kahn**
Elise Knowles	**Cory Andrew Knox**
Matthew Lindahl	**Jessica Giampietro McMackin**
Bob Morgan	**Terry Lee Moseley**
Michael A. O'Brien	**Jeanie T. Oh**

Mark Pananganan	**Kathleen H. Parmelee**
Wil Phan	**Edgar Quiñones**
A.U.B.I.E.	**M.T. Silvia**
Nelson Siu	**Elle Yoko Suzuki**
Andy Thomas	**Jason "JTOP" Topolski**
Chuck Waite	**Jay Weiland**
Ian Westcott	**Adam Wood-Gaines**

POST PRODUCTION

POST PRODUCTION SUPERVISOR	**Paul Cichocki**
SENIOR MANAGER EDITORIAL AND POST PRODUCTION	**Bill Kinder**
PROJECTION	**John Hazelton**
EDITORIAL SERVICES	**Phred Lender** **Andra Smith** **Jeff Whittle**
POST PRODUCTION COORDINATOR	**Courtney Bergin**
ORIGINAL DIALOGUE MIXER	**Doc Kane**
DIALOGUE RECORDIST	**Jeanette Browning**
ADDITIONAL DIALOGUE RECORDING	**Vince Caro** **Charlene Richards** **E.J. Holowicki**

ADDITIONAL ADR VOICE CASTING	**Mickie McGowan**
ADDITIONAL AUSTRALIAN VOICE CASTING	**Ceri Davies**
END CREDIT DESIGN	**Ellen Moon Lee**

POST PRODUCTION SOUND SERVICES BY
SKYWALKER SOUND
A Division of Lucas Digital Ltd., Marin County, California

RE-RECORDING MIXERS	**Gary Rydstrom** **Gary Summers**
SUPERVISING SOUND EDITORS	**Michael Silvers** **Gary Rydstrom**
SOUND EFFECTS EDITORS	**Shannon Mills** **Teresa Eckton** **E. J. Holowicki**
FOLEY EDITOR	**Al Nelson**

ADR EDITOR	**Steve Slanec**
ASSISTANT SOUND DESIGNER	**Dee Selby**
ASSISTANT SUPERVISING SOUND EDITOR	**Stuart McCowen**
FOLEY ARTISTS	**Dennie Thorpe** **Jana Vance**
FOLEY MIXER	**Frank "Pepe" Merel**
FOLEY RECORDIST	**Travis Crenshaw**
MIX TECHNICIANS	**Jurgen Scharpf** **Juan Peralta**
RE-RECORDIST	**Brian Magerkurth**

FACILITIES

Tom Carlisle	Craig Payne
Cherise Miller	Joe Garcia
Aaron Burt	Edgar A. Ochoa
Keith Johnson	Paul Gillis
William de Ridder	Kenny Condit

HUMAN RESOURCES

Sangeeta Prashar	Dawn Haagstad
Lisa Ellis	Shelby Madeleine Cass
Kimberly Adair Clark	Monica VanDis

PIXAR SHORTS

Roger Gould	Osnat Shurer
Bill Polson	Gale Gortney
Steve Bloom	Daniel A. Goodman
Alice Rosen	Alex Orrelle
Chris Vallance	Erin Cass
Omid Amjadi	

PIXAR UNIVERSITY & ARCHIVES

Randy Nelson	Elyse Klaidman
Christine W. Freeman	Elizabeth Greenberg
David R. Haumann	Brandon T. Loose
Andrew Lyndon	

PURCHASING & RELOCATION

Dennis "DJ" Jennings
Jody Giacomini

RENDERMAN PRODUCTS

Ray Davis	Renee Lamri
Jonathan Flack	Dylan Sisson
Lola Gill	Wendy Wirthlin

SAFETY & SECURITY

Keith Kops	Chris Balog
Jonathan Rodriguez	Joni Superticioso
Marlon Castro	Michael Jones
Valerie Villas	Sequoia Blankenship

CRAFT SERVICES

Osvaldo Tomatis	Luis Alarcon-Cisneros
Francisco Figueroa	Loretta Framsted
Candelaria Lozano	Jose Ramirez
Guillermo Segovia	Fernando Contreras
Olga Velaszquez	Maricela Navarro
Meagan Miller	

PRODUCTION BABIES

A.J. IV	Aislinn	Amaey	Ayana
Benjamin	Bergen	Colin	Cynthia
Daniel	Dorri	Ella	Emma
Fiona	Haiden	Hanako	India
Isaac	Jack	Jacob	Jake
Jeremiah	Joshua	Louis	Lucas
Margaret	Matthew	Maximilian	Miles
Nico	Nina	Noah	Oona
Owen	Parker	Rachel	Reese
Riley	Sophia	Sophie	Tallulah
Thomas	Tobias	Yonatan	

SPECIAL THANKS

Adam P. Summers, Fabulous Fish Guy

University of California - Irvine

Aquarium of the Pacific	Steinhart Aquarium
Hal Beral	Maria Elena Magana Cervantes
Roni Douglas, DDS	Dive Makai Charters
Craig Gillespie	Mike Severens Diving

City and County of San Francisco, Public Utilities Commission,
Oceanside Water Pollution Control Facility
Marcia Peck, RDH

CREATED AND PRODUCED AT

Pixar Animation Studios

EMERYVILLE, CALIFORNIA

STEREOSCOPIC 3D

STEREOSCOPIC SUPERVISOR
Bob Whitehill

3D TECHNICAL SUPERVISOR
Daniel McCoy

DIRECTOR OF 3D PRODUCTION
Joshua Hollander

RENDERING LEAD **Reid Sandros**
MANAGERS **Paul McAfee**
Tamsen Mitchell

TECHNICAL & RENDERING

Sean Feeley	Philip Graham	Patrick Guenette	Chris Horne
Jay-Vincent Jones	Joshua Mills	Roxanne Paredes	Jonathan Penney
Nadim Sinno	Eliot Smyrl	Yaa-Lirng Tu	Brett Warne

POST PRODUCTION

SUPERVISOR **Erick Ziegler**
COLORIST **Mark Dinicola**
RE-RECORDING MIXER **Tom Myers**

355

Who's Who in the

MARLIN

FIN FACT: Clownfish

FUN FACT: Nemo's dad, Marlin, fears the world beyond his safe little reef. Marlin is so nervous he thinks that school-age Nemo should wait five or six years before going to school.

FIN FACT: Clownfish

FUN FACT: Nemo has a "lucky" fin that doesn't look like the other one. Nemo is so excited to get to his first day of school, if he can only get Dad to hurry up!

NEMO

FIN FACTS: Flapjack octopus (Pearl), sea horse (Sheldon) and butterfly fish (Tad) are all in Mr. Ray's class at school. They'll make great friends for Nemo once they meet him!

FUN FACTS: Prankster Tad likes to startle Pearl, which makes her let out her ink. So embarrassing! And Sheldon the sea horse has a very inconvenient allergy to, yes, water — but he doesn't let that slow him down!

PEARL

SHELDON

TAD

Ocean Blue!

Learn about the funky fish in Nemo's world!

FIN FACT:
Regal blue tang fish

FUN FACT: Dory is just minding her own business until she meets Marlin, who needs her help! There's just one problem: Dory has no short-term memory, so she can't remember who they're searching for...Elmo? Fabio?

DORY

MR. RAY

FIN FACT: Eagle Ray

FUN FACT: Mr. Ray is the science teacher for the youngest fish in school. There's nothing he likes better than taking a field trip to teach his students something new about the seabed they all live in!

WHO'S WHO
in the
OCEAN BLUE

MARLIN

CLOWN FISH
(Humorii Jellymanicus)

Forced to leave the safety of the reef, Marlin searches for his son. He sees danger everywhere, but keeps on swimming to save Nemo.

DORY

REGAL BLUE TANG FISH
(Memorus Forgeticci)

Dory is Marlin's partner in his search for Nemo. Dory almost never remembers anything, but she can read human and is fearless!

CRUSH

SEA TURTLE *(Dudius Turtlicus)*

150 year old sea turtle that surfs along the EAC (East Australian Current) with his turtle tribe, and his son Squirt.

SQUIRT

SEA TURTLE *(Sweeticci Turtilicus)*

A tiny surfing sea turtle, Squirt rides the current with his dad and the turtle tribe. He's a strong swimmer for his age, and a bit of a show off!

NEMO

GILL

MOORISH IDOL FISH
(Leadirus Escapai)

The leader of the Tank Gang, Gill has a deep scar on his face and a damaged fin. He seems scary, but he befriends Nemo and plots to help him escape.

CLOWN FISH
(Lostimus Clownfisherus)

A young, energetic clownfish captured by a diver, Nemo now finds himself in a dentist's aquarium! Nemo is scared and just wants to see his dad again.

GURGLE

ROYAL GAMMA
(Germaphobius Negatii)

Gurgle is a nervous fish that is a part of the Tank Gang. He is scared by any germs and needs everything to be clean.

JACQUES

CLEANER SHRIMP
(Germus Purgicus)

Jacques is the cleaner of the Tank Gang. He loves to eat the scum and bacteria in the tank. Yum!

DEB

BLACK & WHITE HUMBUG
(Twinicus Reflectus)

Deb likes to talk with her twin sister, and by her twin sister we mean her reflection. She also likes to watch the dentist drill teeth...yikes!

BLOAT

PORCUPINE PUFFERFISH
(Ballooniffi Scaredius)

He may not be as nervous as his friend Gurgle, but it doesn't take much for Bloat to blow up to twice his size!

PEACH

STARFISH *(Clingius Starfisherus)*

Peach is a starfish that clings to the side of the fish tank. She likes watching the dentist work and giving the rest of the fish updates.

BUBBLES

YELLOW TANG *(Crazii Bubblicus)*

The energetic Bubbles likes to babble about his bubbles! He's weirdly obsessed with the bubbles that come out of the treasure chest in the fish tank.

Who's Who IN THE OCEAN

WHEN I WAS TAKEN BY THE DENTIST I WAS *REALLY* SCARED, BUT MY DAD FOUND ME AND HELPED SAVE ME!

I MET A LOT OF *GREAT* FRIENDS ALONG THE WAY. HERE'S EVERYONE THAT I MET OUTSIDE MY... A-MANATEE...AN-ENEMY... *ANEMONE!*

NEMO (me!)

THIS IS ME! MY NAME IS *NEMO!* I'M A CLOWN FISH. I THINK I'M CALLED THAT BECAUSE I'M SO FUNNY.

Dad (Marlin)

THIS GUY THAT LOOKS LIKE ME IS MY *DAD!* HE SWAM ACROSS THE OCEAN TO SAVE ME! HE'S A CLOWN FISH TOO, BUT HE ISN'T VERY FUNNY. BUT I LOVE HIM ANYWAY!

Dory!

DORY IS THE BEST. SHE HELPED MY DAD ON HIS TRIP. SHE ALWAYS KNOWS HOW TO MAKE ME LAUGH. SHE'S REALLY FUN, EVEN THOUGH I HAVE TO KEEP REMINDING HER MY NAME ISN'T "ELMO".

362

BLUE

THE EIGHT TENTACLES IN THIS PICTURE BELONG TO MY FRIEND *PEARL*. SHE IS AN OCTOPUS! WHEN SHE GETS SCARED SHE SHOOTS OUT INK. *GROSS!*

Pearl

Sheldon

SHELDON IS A SEAHORSE. HE IS ALLERGIC TO WATER, AND THAT MAKES HIM SNEEZE A LOT, WHICH IS PRETTY FUNNY!

Tad

TAD IS MY OTHER FRIEND. HE'S REALLY DARING, BUT NOT AS DARING AS ME! HE DIDN'T TOUCH THE BOAT! HE ALSO REALLY LIKES BEING OBNOXIOUS, BUT HE'S STILL MY FRIEND.

Crush

THIS IS THE COOLEST TURTLE EVER, *CRUSH!* HE HELPED MY DAD SWIM ON THE EAST AUSTRALIAN CURRENT (*EAC*). HE'S 150 YEARS OLD AND STILL YOUNG!

Squirt

CRUSH HAS A SON NAMED *SQUIRT*. HE'S JUST AS COOL AS HIS DAD, AND NOW HE GOES TO SCHOOL WITH ME!

Who's Who
IN THE OCEAN BLUE

Gil

THIS SCARY LOOKING FISH, *GIL*, IS THE LEADER OF MY FRIENDS FROM THE TANK. HE NAMED ME "*SHARKBAIT*" AFTER I SWAM THROUGH THE RING OF FIRE. I WASN'T SCARED.

Deb

DEB LOVES WATCHING THE DENTIST DRILL TEETH, AND TALKING TO HER TWIN SISTER *FLO*. I DON'T WANT TO BE MEAN AND TELL HER THAT HER TWIN SISTER IS REALLY JUST HER REFLECTION.

Peach

PEACH LOVES CLINGING TO THE SIDE OF THE TANK BUT SHE ALWAYS FORGETS TO GET OFF THE GLASS TO TALK! HER STAR SHAPE IS WHY SHE IS CALLED A STARFISH!

Bubbles

THIS IS *BUBBLES*. I DON'T REALLY KNOW ANYTHING ABOUT HIM, BESIDES THAT HE *REALLY* LIKES BUBBLES.

part 2

Gurgle

GURGLE IS ALMOST ALWAYS NERVOUS. GERMS SCARE HIM TOO, AND HE FREAKED OUT WHEN HE FOUND OUT I WAS FROM THE OCEAN. **WEIRD!**

Jacques

THIS IS THE TANK'S CLEANER, **JACQUES.** HE IS A SHRIMP. JACQUES HAD TO DISINFECT ME WHEN I GOT INTO THE TANK. HE SPUN ME AROUND REALLY FAST AND I GOT **REALLY** DIZZY!

Bloat

BLOAT HAS AN AWESOME POWER! WHENEVER HE GETS MAD OR SCARED, HE INFLATES TO THE SIZE OF A HUGE BUBBLE! THAT'S WHY HE IS A PUFFERFISH.

THESE ARE THE **SHARKS** THAT MY DAD AND DORY MET WHEN THEY WERE TRYING TO SAVE ME. BRUCE TRIED TO EAT MY DAD! BUT NOW THEY MAKE SURE DORY GETS AROUND SAFELY.

Anchor

Chum

Bruce